Madame Butterfly

THE STORY OF MADAME BUTTERFLY

Madame Butterfly, Giacomo Puccini's tragic grand opera, has a fascinating history. It begins in 1898 when a short story, "Madame Butterfly," by John Luther Long was published in *Century Magazine.* He said that his work was based on a true story and that his sister had met the heroine's grown son in Nagasaki, but that the real Madame Butterfly's suicide attempt had failed.

Two years later, the Broadway impresario and writer, David Belasco, wrote a one-act play based on Long's story, which premiered March 5, 1900, at New York's Herald Square Theater. The play met with great success. Later that year, the play was presented in London, and that is where, on opening night, Puccini first saw it. He was so moved that he was immediately inspired to write an opera based on the story. Luigi Illica and Giusepe Giocosa, who had written the librettos for Puccini's *La Bohème* and *Tosca,* collaborated on the libretto for *Madame Butterfly* as well. The opera premiered at La Scala in Milan, Italy, in 1904, but it was not well received. It was subsequently condensed and divided into two acts and in 1905 made a successful debut at London's Covent Garden. Since then, it has been an enduring favorite with opera lovers around the world.

The tragic story has since been adapted many times. In 1932 Hollywood produced a film version based on the Belasco play. The modern musical *Miss Saigon* shifted the story's setting to the Vietnam war. And most recently, the story served as the inspiration for David Henry Hwang's play and movie, *M. Butterfly.*

Madame Butterfly

The Story of the Opera by
GIACOMO PUCCINI

Illustrated by
RENÁTA FUČÍKOVÁ

Retold by
J. ALISON JAMES

PURPLE BEAR BOOKS
New York

HIGH ON A HILL overlooking the Nagasaki harbor two men were exploring a small house surrounded by a lovely garden. Goro, a Japanese marriage broker, was showing his client, Lieutenant B. F. Pinkerton of the U.S. Navy, the remarkable features of a Japanese house. Walls slid open to become doors. One room could divide into two. The outside doors opened to create a porch.

"You see," said Goro, "the walls come and they go, to suit your whim."

"It's like magic," Pinkerton said, delighted. He was getting this house as part of a deal to buy himself a wife while he was in Japan.

A woman slid open a door, came in, and knelt to bow.

Goro said, "This is the faithful servant to your new wife. Her name is Suzuki, which means gentle breeze."

Pinkerton smiled at the woman, but said, "What a foolish name. I'll call her Scarecrow."

Suzuki said, "You honor me with your smile. A smile smoothes every trouble. Pearls may be won by smiling. Smiles are the gate to heaven."

Pinkerton shook his head, annoyed. "All women are the same when they talk. Such foolishness."

He heard a shout, and stepped outside to see who was coming up the hill.

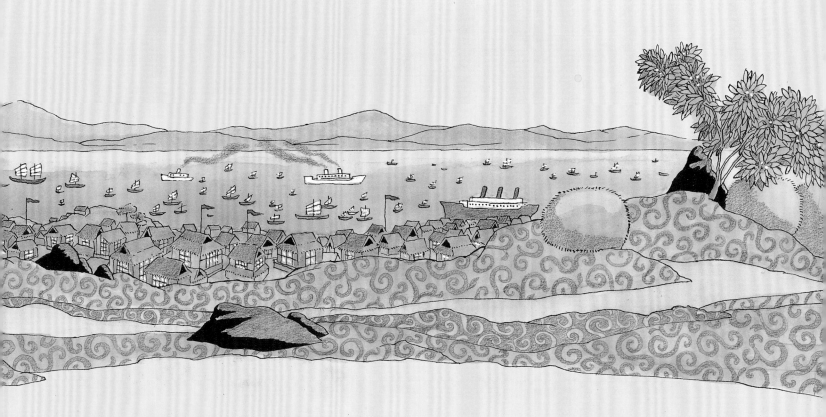

It was his friend Sharpless, the American consul. His face was rosy and sweating, and he stopped to catch his breath. "What a dastardly climb this is."

"Sharpless, come sit in the shade of my little house! Welcome!"

"It certainly is lofty."

"But lovely," Pinkerton said with a laugh. "Goro, bring some refreshment!" He turned to his friend. "This is a home managed by magic." He poured a drink for his friend. "I rented this house for 999 years, with the option to cancel the contract on a month's notice." He slid the door closed behind him. "I do approve of the flexible nature of this country's houses—and contracts!"

"It must be good to get your feet on solid ground after such a time at sea," Sharpless said, looking out over the bay.

"The Yankee travels the whole world over"—Pinkerton stood and spread his arms wide—"scorning all danger. Life is not worth living if I can't win the finest of each country. A lovely house, and the loveliest of maidens."

Sharpless looked at Pinkerton closely. "That's an easy attitude," he said carefully. "But it could prove fatal in the end."

"My marriage contract is the same as for the house," Pinkerton went on, "999 years, with the option to annul on a month's notice."

"And the bride?"

Pinkerton's face shone with delight. "She has entranced me, such innocent charm, so dainty, so fragile. She hovers like a butterfly, just like her name, Cho-Cho."

Sharpless took a sip of his drink. "She came by the consulate the other day," he said. "I heard her speak. Pinkerton, her voice touched my very soul. She spoke of love, pure and true. It would be a shame to tear her tender wings."

Pinkerton laughed. "Oh dear Consul, never fear. Men your age are mournful. It will do no harm to raise those wings to the dizzy heights of love."

Sharpless raised his glass. "To the future, then," he said. "And to your friends and relations at home."

Pinkerton touched his glass with a clink. "And to the day when I'll wed a real wife in America."

Sharpless looked at his friend with disapproval, but before he could say anything, they heard laughing and singing coming up the hill.

It was Cho-Cho-san and her girlfriends. They came up the path, running from flower to flower like a flock of butterflies.

"What a view!"

"Look at the sea!"

"And all the flowers!"

Cho-Cho-san laughed at her friends. "I am the happiest of all girls," she sang. "I am following the sweet call of love."

Her girlfriends laughed and said, "May you also be the luckiest. But before you step through that door, stop and look behind you. Pause and wonder at the beauty of the view."

Pinkerton saw the flock of girls and went to welcome his Butterfly. "I fear the climb has made you weary," he said.

"Not as weary as the lengthy hours waiting to be your bride."

Pinkerton laughed, and introduced Cho-Cho-san to Sharpless.

"Miss Butterfly," said the Consul cordially, "how appropriate a name for such a lovely girl. Are you from Nagasaki?"

"I am," she responded. "My people used to be quite well off."

Sharpless looked interested.

She laughed at herself. "Every beggar has a tale of princely relations, but indeed, I have known riches. However, even the strongest oak releases its roots when convinced by the force of a gale. I had to become a geisha to earn my living."

Sharpless smiled.

"You laugh, but that is how the world is," Cho-Cho-san said defensively.

"Where is your father?" he asked the girl.

"He died," she said. "But I have two uncles. An esteemed Buddhist priest, Bonze, and another uncle, but he is . . ."

Her girlfriends laughed. "Worthless," they said.

Cho-Cho-san tried to hush them. "He is not as thoughtful as Bonze."

Her girlfriends said, "He's married to the bottle."

Pinkerton laughed. "Wonderful. A thinker and a drinker!"

Cho-Cho-san was mortified.

Sharpless gracefully changed the subject. "Tell me, lovely one, what might your age be?"

She laughed with relief. "You try to guess," she said.

"Ten years old?" Sharpless said, joking.

She shook her head. "No, older!"

"Twenty?"

"Younger. I'm fifteen, exactly fifteen."

Sharpless looked at Pinkerton, who was beaming.

Goro the broker came in just then and announced, "It is time for the wedding ceremony. The guests of the bride approach."

Cho-Cho-san's mother and all her relatives were chattering excitedly. Not all of them were pleased that their sweet Butterfly was to marry a strange foreigner.

"Handsome he's not!"

"I've never seen handsomer," Cho-Cho-san said.

"I think he is a fine man," her mother said.

Her cousin called out in a shrill voice, "Goro offered him to me, but I turned him down."

"A likely story," Cho-Cho-san retorted.

"He's worth a lot," one aunt said.

"They'll get divorced," said another.

Pinkerton turned to Sharpless. "Lord, what foolish people."

Sharpless took Pinkerton aside. "I have never seen a maid more lovely or more sweet than your Butterfly. I warn you, be careful, for she trusts you."

Pinkerton turned to his bride. "Come, my sweet, I will show you our house."

"I hope you don't mind," she said shyly. "I've brought a few things."

She showed him the long bulging sleeves of her kimono which she'd used as pockets.

Pinkerton watched, astonished, as she pulled out her personal treasures.

"My silk scarves, a ribbon, a silver buckle, my mirror, and a fan."

Pinkerton pointed to a jar. "What is that?"

"It is carmine to put roses in my cheeks."

Pinkerton looked scornful. "You don't need that. You are lovely as you are."

"I'll throw it away, then," she said, setting it aside.

"And that there?" he asked, pointing to a knife in a sheath.

"That is sacred to me." She set it down carefully. It was the knife her father had used to kill himself when the Mikado ordered him to do so.

Cho-Cho-san took the hands of her beloved Pinkerton. "I must tell you something," she said. "Yesterday I secretly went into the mission and adopted your religion. If I am to be your wife, I will follow you. No one knows what I've done. It was hard, but for you, I can almost forget my family and my faith."

Goro slid open the door. "It's time," he announced.

Pinkerton and his Butterfly went back out to the assembly. The Commissioner read out the lease for the house and for the marriage. Pinkerton signed his name, and then Cho-Cho-san signed hers.

"Oh, Cho-Cho-san," sighed her girlfriends.

She turned to them, smiling. "It is Madame B. F. Pinkerton now."

Sharpless and the Commissioner headed down the hill. They passed Cho-Cho-san's Uncle Bonze hurrying up to the house.

Her other uncle was already drunk. Pinkerton refilled his glass.

"Drink to the happy couple!" Everybody was laughing and talking.

Then they heard a loud voice call out: "Cho-Cho-san!"

Suddenly all was silent. Bonze stood at the door looking furious. "Cho-Cho-san!" he bellowed. "What were you doing at the mission?"

Pinkerton was irritated. "What is that lunatic shouting?"

Bonze went on. "She has renounced her true religion! May your soul perish in eternal torment!"

The guests gasped in horror. "You renounced us? You renouced us? Then we renounce you!" they cried, shunning Cho-Cho-san.

Pinkerton strode to the door and slid it open with a bang. "Leave this place," he cried. "All of you. Here I am master, and I will have no disrespect."

They went off down the hill, buzzing like angry wasps.

Cho-Cho-san burst into tears and held her hands over her ears so she would not have to hear their curses.

Pinkerton took a silk handkerchief and wiped her eyes. "All your relatives and all the priests in Japan are not worth one tear from your lovely eyes."

She turned her face up with a smile. "Indeed?" She reached out and brought his hand to her lips to kiss. He looked confused. Cho-Cho-san said, "I was told that kissing the hand is a sign of highest esteem in your land."

Pinkerton smiled at her. "Indeed." He kissed her small hand. "Evening falls," he said.

"With shadows and quiet," Cho-Cho-san replied. She called for Suzuki to help her into her nightgown, then slid the doors shut and they were alone.

"Now you are a white lily," her husband whispered.

"I am the Goddess of the Moon, coming down the bridge of stars."

"Enchanting this poor mortal."

Cho-Cho-san knelt by her husband. He kissed her hand and her arm. "But sweet Butterfly, you have not yet told me that you love me."

She looked up into his face and said softly, "I fear I may die of my love. You are the world, no, more than the world to me. The moment I first saw you, I loved you. You are so handsome, so very strong, and your laugh, it is so full." She paused. "If you could just love me a little . . . I come from a people accustomed to little, grateful for love that is quiet, but everlasting."

"Ah, my Butterfly," said Pinkerton.

Cho-Cho-san's face clouded. "They say that in your country if a man catches a butterfly he pierces it with a needle and leaves it to perish."

"Cast all fear from your heart," Pinkerton said with passion. "I'll hold you close. See, the world lies sleeping. Come and be mine."

Years passed, three long years since Pinkerton sailed back to his home.

Every day, rain or sun, wind or blowing snow, Cho-Cho-san stood at the edge of the cliff watching for ships in the harbor. Her husband had promised that he would return when the robins built their nest.

Day after day, her maid, Suzuki, knelt before the old gods at her altar praying that her mistress would cease weeping. "Come inside," she begged.

Cho-Cho-san turned to her companion. "Suzuki," she said, "how soon will we starve?"

Suzuki showed her a handful of coins. "This is all we have left. Unless he comes soon . . ."

"He will come," Cho-Cho-san said.

Suzuki shook her head. "I've never heard yet of a foreign husband who returned to his wife."

Cho-Cho-san followed Suzuki up to the house.

"You lack faith," she said. "One fine day, you'll see. A curl of smoke will rise from the horizon, then the ship will appear as if by magic and glide into the harbor. We shall see a small figure in the distance, climbing up the hill to our home. When he reaches the summit, he will call out, 'Butterfly, my sweet one!' I will hide behind the door, in part to tease him, in part not to die of happiness."

Overcome with emotion, Suzuki took Cho-Cho-san in her arms. "You honor him with your love," she said.

A gentleman's voice interrupted their reverie. "Hello?"

It was Sharpless, arriving with Goro and a wealthy merchant named Yamadori.

"Madame Butterfly," Sharpless said.

"Madame Pinkerton," she corrected.

"I've brought a letter," he said, drawing it from his coat.

"From my husband?"

"Yes, from Pinkerton."

"Is he well?"

Sharpless nodded. "He is well."

"Then I am the happiest woman in the world," she exclaimed.

Sharpless twisted the letter in his hands.

Goro impatiently cleared his throat, and Cho-Cho-san turned to Sharpless. "Why are they here with you? My husband had scarcely sailed off when Goro came around trying to get me to marry Yamadori."

Goro said defensively, "She is so poor, and her relatives cast her off!"

"I am already married!"

Goro said, "Desertion gives the right of divorce."

Sharpless said, "I fear I shall never deliver this message. Leave us, Goro."

"Read me the letter," Cho-Cho-san said.

Sharpless opened the paper and started to read: "Dear Friend, I beg you to visit my Butterfly. . . . Those were happy days. Three years have now gone by . . ."

"He, too, has counted!"

"I rely on you to prepare her with tact and caution . . ."

"He's coming?"

Sharpless looked at Cho-Cho-san with a troubled sigh. "Now, tell me. What would you do if he were never to return again?"

Cho-Cho-san froze in place, as if she'd stopped breathing.

Sharpless spoke gently, "I urge you to wed the wealthy Yamadori."

She gasped, "Oh! You've wounded me, you've wounded me deeply." She started to sway. Sharpless held out his arm to support her, but she straightened up. "No, thank you. I felt ready to die, but you see, it's passed, like a ship over the ocean." Sharpless turned to go, his duty done.

"Just wait one moment," Cho-Cho-san said to Sharpless.

Cho-Cho-san left and came back with a little boy, her three-year-old son.

"Look here," she cried. "I might be nothing, but could such a fine boy as this be forgotten?"

Sharpless was moved to tears. "Is that his son?"

"What Japanese baby is born with eyes as azure as the sea, with a nose as straight as the mast of a ship?"

"Has Pinkerton been told? Does he know?"

Cho-Cho-san shook her head. "But you, you could write him. Tell him that his son awaits. A son who has no equal. Then he will hurry back to us, to our home on the hill. Offer the gentleman your hand, son."

The little boy reached out his hand for Sharpless to kiss.

Suzuki came running. "The harbor cannon is booming," she said. "There's a ship coming in!" She handed the telescope to Cho-Cho-san.

"The *Abraham Lincoln!* It's his ship!" She turned excitedly to Sharpless. "Just at the moment you said to forget him, my love proves his loyalty. He's coming! He loves me!"

Cho-Cho-san took her son and ran back to the house to prepare. She dressed him in his finest kimono, and she put on her wedding robes. "Shake the cherry tree," she called to Suzuki, "and sprinkle the blossoms inside. Peach petals, jasmine, and all the wisteria. Leave no flower in the garden. Fill the house with the scent of April."

"The garden will be as desolate as winter," Suzuki protested.

"But spring will spread her sweetness in here."

"There's not a flower left," Suzuki said, her arms full of blossoms.

"Roses will grace our threshold," Cho-Cho-san said, helping Suzuki to scatter the flowers.

Cho-Cho-san held her son in her lap and sat in the doorway to wait. Night fell, and the moon looked down on the little boy asleep in his mother's arms.

Very early the next morning, Sharpless and Pinkerton climbed the hill to the cottage. Suzuki ran outside when she saw them approach. "Hush!" she said. "She is sleeping. She stayed awake all night awaiting your arrival, with the child asleep on her lap."

"How did she know I was here?"

Suzuki said simply, "For three years, no ship has docked in this harbor without Butterfly's notice. Her telescope is always at hand. I'll wake her now."

Pinkerton put his hand out to stop her. "No," he said. "Not yet."

Suzuki saw a lady down in the garden. "Who is she?"

"Hush!" Pinkerton looked around anxiously.

"You'd better tell," Sharpless said.

"She came with me." Pinkerton flushed with embarrassment.

"She's his wife," Sharpless said.

Suzuki raised her arms to heaven, then collapsed in despair.

Sharpless leaned over her and spoke quietly, "We came this early in the morning, Suzuki, so that we could ask your assistance in this delicate situation."

"How could I ever help? How could I?"

Sharpless took Suzuki by the arm and led her away. "It is the child," he said. "Pinkerton's son. We must think of his welfare. In this country, he is a poor child, with no father. In America, he would be raised with wealth and the finest education. We must do what is best for him."

Suzuki cried, "Woe is me! You ask me to go and tell his mother . . ."

"That gentle lady in the garden would be the kindest of mothers to him."

Pinkerton leaned against the doorway, looking at the room strewn with flowers in honor of his arrival. He was lost in a painful reverie. "The very chamber where once we loved is unchanged to this day." He turned to Suzuki. "Call that gentle lady from the garden. Go quickly and bring her here. If Butterfly meets her, then she will learn the cruel truth that I dare not tell."

Suzuki trembled. "All the world is plunged in gloom."

Pinkerton saw his portrait on the altar. "Three years have passed, and Butterfly counted every hour. I cannot stay here. I must go."

Sharpless met him outside. "I warned you, remember? Be careful, I said, for she trusts you."

"Yes," said Pinkerton. "In one sudden moment, I see how heartlessly I acted. I shall never be free from remorse. I cannot bear to stay another moment. Like a coward, let me flee."

Suzuki stood in the garden with the lady, Kate Pinkerton.

Kate spoke gently, entreatingly. "You will tell her, then? You will advise her to trust me?"

Suzuki promised, but her heart was breaking. "She will weep so sadly."

Just then Cho-Cho-san appeared at the door. "Suzuki! Suzuki, where are you?"

"I'm here, in the garden," she said. "I'm coming . . . NO!" She rushed to the staircase to prevent Cho-Cho-san from coming down and seeing the lady.

"He's here, isn't he? I know he's here! Where is he hidden?"

She came around the corner and saw Kate. "Who are you? Why are you here? Why are you weeping?" Slowly the truth began to dawn on her. "No, no. Do not tell me, lest I fall dead at your feet when you say the words. You, Suzuki, whom I trust. Tell me, who is this lady who terrifies me so?"

Kate responded, "Through no fault of my own, I am the cause of your distress. Oh, pray, forgive me." She reached out her hand to Cho-Cho-san.

"No. Do not touch me." She spoke with cool calm. "How long ago did he marry you?"

"One year." She hesitated, then spoke, "Will you let me care for the child? I will tend him lovingly, and give him all he could want."

Cho-Cho-san was frozen with horror.

"It is hard, I am sure, but I entreat you, do it for his own good."

Cho-Cho-san's face was as pale as death. "There is nothing. All is over."

"Can you not forgive me?" Kate implored.

"Of all that lives beneath the blue vault of the sky, there can be none happier than you. May you not be saddened by my plight. Do one thing for me, though. Please will you tell him . . . that peace will come to me?"

Kate breathed with relief. "May I kiss your hand?"

Cho-Cho-san shrank back. "No. Not that. I pray you. Now go, leave me."

"But can he have his son?"

"His son I will give him, if he will come himself to fetch the boy. Climb this hill one hour from now. His son will be ready."

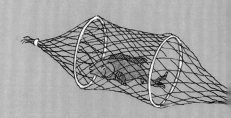

Cho-Cho-san withdrew to her room. She pulled out her father's knife and bowed before it reverently. She read the inscription aloud: "Death with honor is better than life with dishonor." She withdrew the blade.

Behind her, Suzuki slid open the door and pushed the boy inside.

Cho-Cho-san dropped the knife and ran to her son. "Oh, you, you, you! My beloved adored boy, my fairest flower. Though you must never know, it is for you that I will die, so you may go away across the ocean. For if I were alive I could never let you go, I love you so. Farewell, beloved, farewell. Go, go play."

She sat her little boy on a stool and gave him a toy. She tied a silk scarf around his eyes so he would not see what she had to do. Then she took up the dagger and went behind a screen.

The knife fell to the floor with a soft sound.

With a large white scarf wound around her neck, Cho-Cho-san crawled into the room and stretched out her hand for her son.

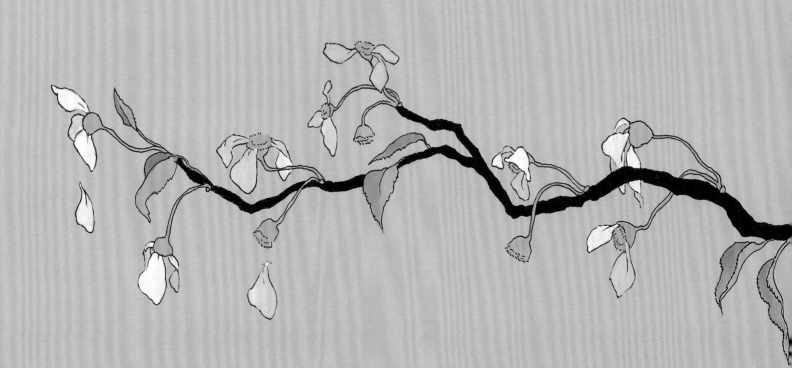

"Butterfly! Butterfly! Butterfly!" Pinkerton pushed open the door and rushed into the room.

Cho-Cho-san feebly raised her head, pointed to her son, and fell back, into her husband's arms.

Pinkerton clasped her to him. Too late, he realized the full weight of her love. He kissed her cold cheek and wept.

FIRST PUBLISHED IN TAIWAN IN 2004 BY GRIMM PRESS.
FIRST ENGLISH-LANGUAGE EDITION PUBLISHED IN 2005
BY PURPLE BEAR BOOKS INC., NEW YORK.
FOR MORE INFORMATION ABOUT OUR BOOKS
VISIT OUR WEBSITE, PURPLEBEARBOOKS.COM

LIBRARY OF CONGRESS CATALOGING-IN-PUBLICATION
DATA IS AVAILABLE.
THIS EDITION PREPARED BY CHESHIRE STUDIO.

ISBN 1-933327-04-9 (TRADE EDITION)
10 9 8 7 6 5 4 3 2 1
ISBN 1-933327-08-1 (LIBRARY EDITION)
10 9 8 7 6 5 4 3 2 1
PRINTED IN TAIWAN